For Josie

Special thanks to Sarah Levison

ORCHARD BOOKS

First published in 2018 by The Watts Publishing Group

1 3 5 7 9 10 8 6 4 2

A CIP catalogue record for this book is available from the British Library.

ISBN 978 1 40835 180 2

Printed and bound in China

The paper and board used in this book are made from wood from responsible sources.

Orchard Books
An imprint of Hachette Children's Group
Part of The Watts Publishing Group Limited
Carmelite House, 50 Victoria Embankment, London EC4Y 0DZ

An Hachette UK Company
www.hachette.co.uk
www.hachettechildrens.co.uk

Rarity's
Friendship Lesson

ORCHARD

Fluttershy loves animals. Her cutie mark is three pink butterflies.

Rainbow Dash is a fast Pegasus pony. Her cutie mark is a cloud with a rainbow lightning bolt.

Rarity is a glamorous Unicorn. Her cutie mark is three blue diamonds.

Twilight Sparkle is learning all about magic. Her cutie mark is a pink star.

Pinkie Pie loves to make everyone laugh. Her cutie mark is three bouncing balloons.

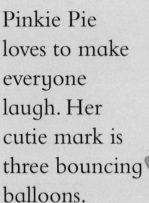

Applejack works on a farm. Her cutie mark is three red apples.

Princess
Celestia is
the ruler of
all Equestria!
She is beautiful,
kind and wise.
Her cutie mark
is a sun.

The
Wonderbolts
are the best
flyers in
Equestria.

Contents

Part One: Practice Makes Perfect

Part Two: Rarity's Wings

Part Three: Winner Takes It All

Part One
Practice Makes Perfect

Chapter One

The Sonic Rainboom

Rainbow Dash was flying in the sky high above Ponyville. She performed lots of exciting twists and loops. Her friend Fluttershy flew nearby, cheering her on.

Rainbow Dash was

practising for the Best Young
Flyer Competition. The contest
was taking place in Cloudsdale,
a city high up in the clouds.

"Now it's time for my best
move, the sonic rainboom!"
Rainbow Dash cried.

The sonic rainboom was the toughest flying move of all. Rainbow Dash was the only pony who had ever made a sonic rainboom, and she had only been able to do it once!

Fluttershy watched as Rainbow tried to do the move. But Rainbow Dash made a mistake and tumbled down through the air. She landed in the Golden Oak Library. Rainbow Dash's friends Rarity, Twilight Sparkle, Pinkie Pie and Applejack were all there.

They were surprised to see her.

"Hey ..." groaned Rainbow Dash. "I was practising my routine for the Best Young Flyer Competition."

Pinkie Pie jumped up and down in excitement.

"Oh, I wish we could come and cheer you on!" said Pinkie.

But Pinkie Pie, Applejack, Twilight and Rarity couldn't go to Cloudsdale because they didn't have wings like Rainbow Dash and Fluttershy.

Rainbow Dash wished her friends could come. She was also worried that she couldn't make another sonic rainboom. "Well, I'm going to rest up for the big day," she said to her friends, and flew away.

Chapter Two

A Special Spell

"I think Rainbow Dash is nervous about her performance," Rarity said.

"I wish we could go to Cloudsdale and cheer her on!" Pinkie Pie said. "If only we all had wings!"

Then Rarity had an idea.
"Twilight, do you know a spell
that would give us wings?" she
asked. "Then we could travel
to Cloudsdale together and
support Rainbow Dash in her
competition."

Twilight Sparkle searched through her magic books and found a spell that would give the ponies wings for a few days. "Hmmm, it looks like a difficult spell," she said. "I need to test it on one pony."

"You can try it on me,
darling!" said Rarity. "I
hope it works! I want to go
to Cloudsdale to cheer on
Rainbow Dash!"

Twilight Sparkle took a deep
breath and concentrated hard.

Magic flowed from her horn
and surrounded Rarity. Then
there was a huge flash. But had
the spell worked?

Chapter Three

Surprise in the Sky!

Later that day, Fluttershy flew up to Cloudsdale. There were flying ponies everywhere!

She saw Rainbow Dash. But before she could get to her friend, three mean ponies suddenly appeared.

They told Rainbow Dash
that they didn't believe she
could make a sonic rainboom.
They even called her Rainbow
Crash. Kind Fluttershy stood
up for her friend, but Rainbow
Dash still felt very sad.

"Those ponies are right," she said. "I won't be able to do the sonic rainboom, and everyone is going to watch me get it wrong!"

Just then, Fluttershy saw something very surprising.

It was Rarity! She was flying in the sky, and she had the most beautiful wings! Rainbow Dash was also very surprised to see Rarity flying.

"Don't you just love my beautiful wings?" Rarity said.

"Twilight made them for me! We've come to cheer for you, Rainbow Dash!"

A hot-air balloon appeared through the clouds. Inside it were Applejack, Pinkie Pie and Twilight Sparkle.

"The spell I used to make Rarity's wings was very tricky, so I found another spell for us," Twilight explained. "We can walk on clouds instead."

Pinkie Pie jumped out of the hot-air balloon and bounced from cloud to cloud. "Wheeeeee!"

Rainbow Dash was so pleased that her friends were there! Maybe the competition wouldn't be so bad after all.

Part Two
Rarity's Wings

Chapter Four

Weather Worries

Rainbow Dash was very
pleased that all her friends
had come to Cloudsdale.
She showed them around the
whole city. The friends gasped
in wonder at the beautiful
buildings made of clouds.

But Rarity was more interested in looking at her new wings. And lots of other ponies were also saying how lovely her wings were!

Rarity flew around, showing off her wonderful new wings.

"Be careful, Rarity," Twilight Sparkle warned. "Your magic wings are very delicate."

But Rarity didn't listen to Twilight. She flew around everywhere, showing off her new wings to everyone.

In the Weather Factory, Rainbow Dash showed her pony pals where delicate snowflakes were made. But Rarity flapped her new wings too hard and made all the snowflakes into a snowstorm!

Next was the rainbow room, but the mean ponies were there. "It's Rainbow Crash!" they teased. Even though they were mean to Rainbow Dash, they were very nice to Rarity. "Your wings are amazing," they said.

"Rainbow Crash, you must wish your wings looked like those ones!"

Rarity flew up in the air with a big smile. She didn't see how sad her friend Rainbow Dash was looking.

Chapter Five

Rarity Shows Off

"Don't listen to those mean
ponies, I know you're going
to win the competition!"
Fluttershy whispered to
Rainbow Dash. But Rainbow
felt worried all over again. She
also felt hurt that Rarity had

laughed with the mean ponies.

"I'm doomed," Rainbow Dash said. "I can't make a sonic rainboom and I only have boring wings!"

Twilight Sparkle and Applejack were worried.

They were supposed to be making Rainbow Dash feel better, not worse!

"Rarity, we're supposed to be making Rainbow Dash feel happy, not sad. Put your wings away and stop showing off!"

Twilight Sparkle said to Rarity, as she fluttered around showing her magical wings to a big crowd of ponies.

"How can you ask me to put away my perfect wings!" cried Rarity.

"You should enter the Best Young Flyer Competition!" one of the ponies said.

"Yes, I will enter the competition!" agreed Rarity. "Then everyone will have a chance to see my wings!"

Rarity had forgotten that she was in Cloudsdale to support Rainbow Dash.

Chapter Six

Competition Time

"The competition is going to be a disaster," cried Rainbow Dash. "I can't make a sonic rainboom, and everyone seems to be more interested in Rarity's amazing new wings than in me!"

But it was time for the Best Young Flyer Competition to start. Princess Celestia was there to watch and so were the Wonderbolts. The Wonderbolts were the best flyers in Equestria and Rainbow Dash's heroes.

The pony who won would spend a day training with the Wonderbolts. Rainbow Dash wanted to win that prize more than anything! But she still felt very nervous. She decided that she would be the last pony to

perform her routine.

Rarity was taking a very long time to do her hair and makeup! She wanted to look the best she could. With her beautiful wings, she was sure she'd be the star of the show.

Rarity and Rainbow Dash were both so late they were told they would have to perform at the same time.

Part Three
Winner Takes It All

Chapter Seven

Sun Burn

Rainbow Dash and Rarity came out into the arena at the same time. Rarity started a delicate dance that showed off her perfect wings. Rainbow Dash tried her best to perform her speedy flying routine.

But she couldn't concentrate and she didn't do a good job.

For the final part of her display, Rarity decided she would fly up to the sun and let the light shine through her beautiful wings!

"Everyone will be talking about this for years!" she cried, flying up to the burning sun.

At first, it looked like Rarity's plan was going to work. She flew close to the sun and opened up her wings.

There were beautiful patterns as the sunlight shone through her wings. But it was so hot that her magic wings disappeared. With a loud scream Rarity started to fall towards the ground.

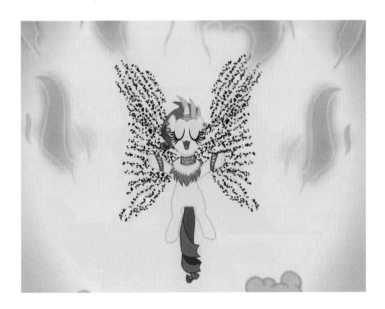

The Wonderbolts tried to reach her, but Rarity's hooves knocked them out of the way. Rarity was in trouble!

Chapter Eight
Rarity's Rescue!

"Hold on, Rarity, I'm coming!" shouted Rainbow Dash. Saving her friend was much more important than doing well in the competition.

Rainbow Dash hurtled down to the ground at top speed.

She flew closer and closer to Rarity. Would she reach her in time?

"I can't look!" cried Fluttershy.

Rainbow Dash flew faster than she had ever flown before.

All she was thinking about was saving Rarity. As she got close to her friend, Rainbow Dash was flying so fast she made a sonic rainboom! The light from the beautiful rainbow covered the watching ponies.

Rainbow Dash managed to catch Rarity just before she hit the ground – and carried her back up to Cloudsdale.

Everyone was cheering with delight at Rainbow Dash's amazing performance. Everyone thought Rainbow Dash was really brave.

"Thank you, Rainbow Dash. You saved my life!" sobbed Rarity.

"And I flew super fast and made a sonic rainboom!

This was the best day EVER!"
cried Rainbow Dash, happily.

Chapter Nine
The Right Winner

"I'm so sorry I behaved badly," Rarity told her friends. "And I'm sorry for how I treated you, Rainbow Dash. I forgot I was meant to be supporting you."

Princess Celestia flew down to see the ponies.

"Rainbow Dash really is the best flyer in Equestria!" Rarity told the princess.

"I know she is," Celestia smiled. "And that's why she's the winner of the Best Young Flyer Competition!"

Rainbow Dash flew around the arena in delight!

"I've learnt a very important friendship lesson today," Rarity said to Princess Celestia.

"Well done, Rarity," said Princess Celestia.

And with that the ponies cheered for their friend Rainbow Dash. Rarity cheered louder than anyone else!

The End

There's lots of colouring, sticker and activity fun with My Little Pony!

Dress-Up Fun
Sticker Activity Book

Pinkie Pie's Party
Sticker and Activity Book

Super Sticker Scenes

Bumper Wipe-Clean Activity Fun

Friendship Fun
Colouring Book

Colouring Fun

Princess Ponies
Sticker and Activity Book

Super Sparkly
Sticker Fun

Holiday Fun
Sticker and Activity Book